An Orion paperback
First published in Great Britain in 2006
by Orion Books Ltd
Orion House, 5 Upper St Martin's Lane,
London WC2H 9EA

1 3 5 7 9 10 8 6 4 2

A CIP catalogue record for this book
is available from the British Library.

ISBN-13: 978-0-75287-954-3
ISBN-10: 0-75287-954-5

Typeset by SX Composing DTP, Rayleigh, Essex

Printed and bound in Great Britain by
Clays Ltd, St Ives plc

www.orionb

Star Sullivan

Maeve Binchy

BY MAEVE BINCHY

Light a Penny Candle
Echoes
London Transports
Dublin 4
The Lilac Bus
Firefly Summer
Silver Wedding
Circle of Friends
The Copper Beech
The Glass Lake
Evening Class
Tara Road
Scarlet Feather
Quentins
Nights of Rain and Stars

Aches & Pains (non-fiction)

To dearest Gordon with all my love

Star Sullivan

CHAPTER ONE

MOLLY SULLIVAN SAID THAT the new baby was a little star. She was no trouble at all and she was always smiling.

Shay Sullivan said the new baby was a star picker of winners, it pointed its little fist at the horse on the list that was going to win.

So she became known as Star and everyone forgot that her real name was Oona. Star forgot it herself. At school when they read out the roll-call they always said, 'Star Sullivan?' On the street where she lived people would shout over to her, 'Star, would you do us a favour and mind the baby for me?' or run to the corner shop, or help to fold a big tablecloth, or find a puppy that had gone missing. Star Sullivan had a head of shiny copper hair, a ready smile and a good nature, and she did everything that she was asked to.

There were three older than Star in the family and none of them had her easy, happy ways.

1

There was Kevin, he was the eldest. He said he was going to work in a gym, eventually own his own sports club, and he fought with his father about everything.

There was Lilly, who was going to be a model one day and had no interest in anyone except herself.

There was Michael, who spent more time in the head teacher's office than he did in the classroom. He was always in trouble over something.

And then there was Star.

Often Star asked her mother, would there be another baby coming? Someone she could push in a pram up and down Chestnut Street. But her mother said no, definitely not. The angel who brought babies had brought enough to number 24. It would be greedy to ask for more.

So Star pushed other people's babies and played with their cats. On her own.

Chestnut Street was a lovely place to play, because it was shaped like a horseshoe and there was a big bit of grass in the middle beside some chestnut trees.

Some of the people who lived there went to great trouble to keep it looking nice. Others just sat there at night and drank lager and left the cans.

There were other children around but Star was shy. She was afraid to go up to a group playing in case they told her to go away. Everyone else looked as if they were having a good time already so she hung about on the edges and never joined them.

Molly Sullivan was glad that her youngest child was so little trouble. There was too much else to think about. Like Shay's gambling, for instance. He said he was doing it for them all, for the family. He was going to have a big win and take them all on a holiday. Foolish decent Shay, who worked in the kitchens of a big hotel and dreamed of becoming the kind of man who could stay there as a guest. As if any of them except little Star would ever want to go on a family holiday, were he ever to afford it!

And Molly Sullivan worried about her work. She worked shifts in a supermarket where they were very busy and she was run off her feet. She had to keep a big smile on her face and be very quick lest they think she was too old and let her go.

She worried about Kevin. He was grumbling

3

because he was still picking up towels and taking the bookings at the Sports Club. He thought he should have been made a trainee manager by now.

Molly worried about Lilly, too. She worked far too hard, endless hours at a telesales centre, so that she could pay for further model training courses. She was thinner than ever and ate practically nothing at home. Of course she said they had *huge* lunches in the office, which was odd, as Molly didn't think they had a kitchen there. But then Lilly wouldn't say it unless it was true.

And as for Michael! Well, he was a worry from dawn till dusk. His teachers said that he would barely be able to read by the time he left school. He had no interest in any subject. His future looked very bleak indeed.

So it was always consoling to think about little Star with her eager face. Star who had never caused any trouble to anyone. Star wore Lilly's old clothes with pleasure, and even the T-shirts of the two boys. She didn't ask for anything new.

At school they said she didn't find the work easy and was always very anxious if asked to read or recite a poem. She was a kind child, they said, and if anyone else fell in the playground or got sick, Star Sullivan was always there to help. Maybe she might be a nurse one day, suggested Miss Casey, one of the teachers. Molly was pleased. It would be lovely to have a nurse in the family after the two dreamers who thought they were going to run a sports club or parade down a catwalk, and Michael who might well end up in gaol.

Shay said that Star would make some man a terrific wife, because she was so interested in things instead of just sighing and shrugging her shoulders like the rest of the family. He would explain the odds to her and the difference it made if the going was hard or soft, and the weights the jockeys had added, and how to do an Accumulator or a Yankee. She would ask bright questions, too, and once or twice had prevented him from doing something foolish.

'Only once or twice?' Molly had said, wearily.

'That's what I mean,' Shay said. 'She doesn't make bitter, harsh remarks like you do, like everyone else does. She's a little treasure, Star is.'

And Kevin never said a word against her. She

helped him clean his shoes and asked all about the people who came to use the fitness machines in the gym. And she never took any of Lilly's things, just admired them. She never told her mother that Lilly stuffed uneaten food in the back of the dressing-table drawers in the room they shared.

Even Michael had a soft spot for Star. She didn't carry horrible news back from school about him. In fact, she told her parents that he was getting on much better than he actually was and sometimes she tried to help him with his homework, even though she was two years younger.

So Star got to the grown-up age of thirteen full of hope and dreams and sure that the world could be all right if you just believed that it was. They didn't realise at home that this was the way she felt, because number 24 Chestnut Street was not a house where there was time for people to sit and think about the Meaning of Life.

And there was always a drama, like when Molly had the money saved for a new washing machine, and Shay put it all on a greyhound that was still hopping on three legs around Shelbourne Park.

Or the time when Lilly had fainted at her telesales office and had been sent home with advice from a doctor that she take greater care of herself, as she was starting to show signs of an eating disorder.

Or Kevin's latest row with his father about not having had enough money to send him to a proper private school where he could have learned PE. And Michael was suspended from school for a whole term and was only taken back because Molly went to the head teacher and pleaded with him.

At Star's school they were just relieved that Star had a smile instead of the constant sulk and sneer that so many of the girls wore all day. Star did not have a pierced nose or lip, saving endless hours of argument. If someone was needed to help clean up the classroom, or put out the chairs, or change the water in the flower vases, Star would do it without a seven-minute protest, which the teachers would get from the rest of the class.

When Molly came in on the parent–teacher days they told her that Star was a great girl, no trouble at all, which Molly knew already. Star wanted to be a nurse, and the teachers would say, sure she would be a wonderful nurse, and with a little extra help there was no reason why she couldn't do that. Was there a chance she could have private teaching? Sadly Molly shook her head. Not a chance in the world, the money they had barely covered things as they were.

Could the older children help possibly, Miss Casey wondered. Molly thought glumly about the three older children and said, not really, to be honest.

Miss Casey didn't even go down the path of asking if the parents would help. A neighbour maybe? They all led very busy lives of course but there *was* a nice neighbour called Miss Mack in Chestnut Street. She was blind, people did go to visit her and read to her, and it was said that she helped and encouraged them, so maybe it might work for Star.

'Tell Star she'd be doing the old lady a kindness, that will make her go to see her,' Miss Casey said.

Star found that Miss Mack was very interested in Star's school books.

'Could you read me again the bit about the French Revolution that you read last week? It's very exciting, isn't it?'

'Is it, Miss Mack?'

'Oh yes, we have to think about why those lords and ladies around the court of the king were so stupid that they didn't see what was going on in the country and how poor the great mass of the people were. Or *did* they see and not care? That's what I want to know.'

'I think they were just blind, Miss Mack,' Star said, trying to excuse people as usual.

Then she realised what she had said. 'I mean . . . I'm so sorry, Miss Mack.'

'Child, it doesn't matter at all. I *am* blind, I wasn't always blind, it's only a word, and in my case it has to do with muscles and things in my eyes wearing out. I recall perfectly what you looked like when you were a little baby. But in the case of the nobles, that was a different kind of blindness, where they wouldn't see what would disturb them.'

Star was so relieved that her blunder had not caused a scene or an upset that she rushed to speak. 'I suppose we all do that, Miss Mack, try not to think about bad things, don't we? You know, try to stop fights and rows and things. I mean, if I had been alive at the French Revolution, I'd have tried to stop them fighting.

I wouldn't have let them have the thing that chopped people's heads off. And the heads falling into baskets.'

'The guillotine, Star. Say it now, say it slowly several times and you'll never forget it.'

Star said it obediently.

'Did you want to stop people fighting, Miss Mack?'

'Yes, I did, but I learned that people only do what they want to do. In the end that's how it is. I think we are stronger if we sort of accept that. It lets us get on with our own lives.'

'But aren't other people our own lives, Miss Mack?'

'They are, child. They are of course.'

Miss Mack sighed. Star didn't have to tell her of all the problems there were at Number 24. Everyone knew. Shay, who would gamble his last euro on anything that was offered. Molly, who was worn out from working and saving. Young Kevin, moody and unhappy, kicking stones around the road. Lilly, who had starved herself to become a model and now had an eating disorder. Michael, who was as near to a criminal as a fifteen-year-old could be. Thoughtful little Star, with the pensive eyes and the long shiny hair, who worried about them all from morning to night.

It was Star's fourteenth birthday and a lot of things happened that day. The Hale family moved in next door into number 23. It had been empty for six months because the Kelly family, who had never visited poor old Mr Kelly who used to live there, had fought over what should be done about it. In the end they sold it quickly to the Hales. Star watched them arrive as the removal van was being unpacked, hoping there might be a girl her age. She didn't have many friends at school, as the other girls thought she was a bit boring.

But no sign of a schoolgirl. A man, his wife, who looked a lot younger than him, a grey-hound and finally, last out of the van, a boy – well, a man nearly . . . Someone about eighteen or nineteen. Star watched in amazement as he took out of the van his guitar and his racing bike. She saw how he pushed his damp hair away from his face. She saw the sweat on his dark grey T-shirt as he helped to carry in the furniture. Could he be part of the removal company or was he part of the family? As the

11

minutes went by, she found herself hoping that he was part of the family. Imagine having a boy next door. A boy who looked like that!

Soon she could bear it no longer and went down to stand at her front door.

'Hallo,' she said as he passed by, carrying a table.

'Hallo there.' He had a great smile.

'I'm Star Sullivan,' she said. Her heart was beating fast. Never had she found the courage to talk to a good-looking boy like this. Somehow this was different.

'Well, hallo, Star Sullivan. I'm Laddy Hale,' he said.

Laddy Hale. She said the words with wonder. It was such a great name. She had better go now before she said something stupid and made him lose that big smile.

Star was in love.

CHAPTER TWO

LIFE WENT ON AS usual in Chestnut Street for everyone except Star.

Molly got more hours working in the supermarket, which was just as well because Shay had a huge loss on what was meant to be a sure thing at Fairyhouse Racecourse.

Kevin had had a row with the gym and was now working in a big hotel, partly in their fitness centre but also partly as a hotel porter, which he didn't like at all. He hid in case he ever met anyone he knew.

Lilly had a fall coming home from work and when the ambulance took her to hospital the doctors called Molly in and showed her Lilly's arms, which were like thin sticks. The girl was in danger of dying from lack of food, they said.

Michael was in deep trouble. He had been part of a gang who stole sixty pairs of jeans from a store and were caught selling them at a market. He was on probation this time, but the next offence would land him in custody.

It was not a house where it was ever easy to study or do homework, but now it was worse than ever. Star couldn't sit in the living room because her father and Kevin were always arguing over work or what to watch on the television. The kitchen table was always covered in cheap vegetables, which her mother would buy at the end of the day in the supermarket. Every night she would make a different soup with them. Every night Lilly refused to eat it because it was full of fat. Michael was watched like a hawk. If he so much as stepped outside the front door, half the family was after him, getting him back.

And all the time the Hales lived next door. Mr Hale went out at seven-thirty every morning to his job in a garden centre, where he had to open up, do the watering and leave out the small plants that might tempt workers on their way to their offices.

Star had learned all this slowly over months and months of trying to get to know Laddy's family. The young woman that she had thought was his mother wasn't his mother at all, she discovered, just a friend of the family. Laddy's mother had long gone. Took off one day and never came back. The woman's name was Biddy. She worked in a pub so she left later in the morning and came back later at night.

Laddy came and went. Star had asked him what he did and he said, a bit of this, a bit of that. She had nodded as if it had meant something to her.

Star's mother didn't really approve of the Hales. They had a great garden, yes, sure, but then why wouldn't they? Owen Hale, the father, often brought a lot of stuff home with him of an evening. Then that Biddy was no better than she should be, half Owen's age for one thing, and she went out to work dressed like a tart in the late mornings. And the son, trouble if ever she saw it.

Star's dad did not agree. Owen Hale was a decent skin, glad to buy a pint and talk up a race; the young one – the friend of the family with the big chest – was a fine looker; and the boy was only a kid and at least he had a smile on him, which was more than you could say for Kevin.

Kevin didn't notice the Hale family much,

15

because he had too much to think about. The hotel manager had told him that he was to think of himself as a hotel porter with duties in the fitness centre, nothing more, nothing less. He could take it or leave it. There were a lot of Eastern Europeans who would die for the job *and* have a smile on their faces.

It worried Star to see her brother so upset. She asked her two friends, Miss Casey at school and Miss Mack over at number 3, what they thought about it all. These were women who could keep secrets. They both said that Kevin shouldn't give up the day job, but he could always look around for jobs in gyms and spas at the same time.

Lilly didn't really notice the Hale family either. She was beside herself because she said that rolls of fat had appeared around her ribs. Star couldn't see them or feel them, and she knew that Lilly was vomiting every day to get rid of the food that their mother made her eat.

Michael was in a world of his own as he needed to find somewhere to hide boxes of CDs and DVDs very quickly. He knew he could tell Star about it as she wouldn't inform on him. Not that she was any help. She just sat there listening to him. Her mind miles away.

'Oh, go on, Star, say something. What do you think?' Michael asked.

Star hadn't been listening.

'What are you thinking about?'

'I was thinking about Laddy Hale next door,' she said without meaning to.

Michael smiled slowly. 'That's not a bad idea. I'm sure he'd help,' he said, and was gone before Star could stop him.

She watched in horror from the upstairs window as she saw her brother make shapes with his hands, showing the size of the boxes. Laddy seemed to be nodding and agreeing. Then she saw Michael rush back home and collect four huge boxes, which he and Laddy carried into the Hales' shed.

Star was torn by this. It was good that Laddy had formed some kind of bond with her brother, true. That brought them all closer together. But it was bad if Laddy was prepared so easily to handle stolen goods. Very bad.

The very next day the police came around, acting, they said, on information received. They had a warrant to search number 24 Chestnut Street for stolen CDs and DVDs.

They found nothing.

17

Laddy was in his garden cleaning his racing bike as they left. He raised his head to look as any interested neighbour might. Star bit her lip as she watched.

Michael was outraged. 'How *dare* they come and hassle us like this? It's just a case of giving a dog a bad name, isn't it, Mam? Isn't it, Dad?' His parents shook their heads, dazed with relief that this time, at any rate, Michael had not been at the centre of some crime.

Only Star knew where the stuff was hidden. She tried to put it out of her mind but she had not reckoned on Michael. Michael now thought of Laddy as his partner in crime.

'He's an all right fellow, that Laddy,' Michael said. He said this often and for no reason.

'What does he actually *do* for a living?' Star's mother would ask.

'A bit of this and a bit of that,' Star heard herself saying.

'Exactly.' Michael looked at her with approval.

Star asked her mother to get any nice shampoo that might be going cheap at the supermarket. Molly was surprised. Unlike the rest of her family Star never asked for anything.

'Something that would make my hair less like a brown mouse,' Star suggested.

'You have lovely hair, Star. Real chestnut colour,' her mother replied.

'Whatever,' Star said, not believing it for a moment.

And then Star bought a skinny, tight red top with her pocket money. Usually she bought treats for Kylie, the cat at number 20, or chocolate biscuits for Miss Mack at number 3. This was not her usual spending pattern.

And then Molly saw Star looking at the boy next door. And understood everything.

There had been no serious Young Love in the Sullivan family before this. Kevin was too busy thinking about his career to have time for more than casual girlfriends. Lilly had no time for fellows, what with work and studying the way models walked and watching every single thing she put into her mouth. It was just as well that young Michael didn't seem to be involved with girls, he had caused so much trouble in everything else he had done.

So it was Star, the baby, who was the first to fall in love. Molly wished it had been with someone younger and less racy than Laddy Hale. And someone more likely to love Star in return. Star was lovely but she was a child, and even Molly would admit that she was a bit unworldly. This boy was handsome, but quick and sharp, too quick for little Star.

So the girl's heart would likely be broken, but then Molly knew that happened to everyone somewhere along the line. Either very quickly at the start, or slowly over the years. That was what Shay had done to her. She had hoped for such a different life than the one they had now. If she had known that Shay would never hold down a decent job and that *she* would have to support the family by working in a supermarket all her life, she might have had second thoughts about marrying him. Still her shift was just about to start, so she could spend no more time worrying about it.

Star tried to get to know Biddy as a way into the family. It wasn't easy. Biddy wasn't a person who got to know her neighbours. Star told her about Miss Mack and how she had gone blind.

'Really?' was all that Biddy said.

So Star moved on to happier stories . . . To

Agnes the fortune-teller, who lived in number 26 together with Melly, and about Bucket Maguire, the window cleaner in number 11 who was so nice to everyone and cleaned Miss Mack's windows for her for free, even though she couldn't see out of them.

'You know everyone in the road,' Biddy said.

'Well, I was born here so I've been here for ages. It's different for you, you'll *get* to know them.' Star didn't want to accept too much praise.

'And every little thing about their business to talk and gossip about, too,' Biddy said.

Now Star knew that it wasn't really praise. Her face got very red.

'Sorry,' she said. 'I thought you'd be interested since you've come to live here, I suppose.'

Biddy looked hard at her. The girl meant no harm. 'Sure I am. Thanks, Star. You're OK,' she said. And Star smiled.

Michael said that Laddy was great, and that he knew everyone in town. The family jumped on him with questions about Laddy.

Lilly said she was sure he only knew criminals and wide boys – was that the case?

21

Kevin asked, did he know anyone selling sports equipment?

Star asked, had he a girlfriend?

But Michael knew no answers to all these questions.

Molly went on doing the ironing and said nothing.

Shay said nothing because he wasn't in the conversation. He was taking notes on what would be the bet of all time. It was just a matter of getting the stake. The money to invest.

Miss Casey told them she was leaving at the end of the term.

Star was upset. 'I thought you would be here for ever, Miss Casey,' she said.

'I know, that was the way it was starting to look,' Miss Casey agreed.

'Where are you going?'

Star was the only child who cared. The others were more interested in who would come after her. Would it be someone strict or someone easy?

So Miss Casey told her. She was going to live in Spain with a gentleman she had met. She would work in his café and sell jewellery with him.

'Oh, Miss Casey, isn't that *wonderful*? You're getting married,' Star said, her eyes shining at the romance of it all.

'Not exactly married, Star, but the next best thing,' Miss Casey said.

'Can I write to you there, Miss Casey?'

Miss Casey did not reply but there was a look in her eyes that Star had seen before in people. Somehow in some way she had gone too far, asked too much.

And Star knew that she shouldn't tell anyone about the teacher's plans. But oddly she told Laddy Hale a few weeks later. He was polishing his bike in the front garden as usual.

'It's very clean already,' Star said, admiring it.

'It's not about getting it clean, it's about having it shining,' Laddy said. 'There's a race at the weekend.'

'Do they give you extra marks for a shining bike?' Star asked.

'No, Star, they don't.' He was short with her.

So she decided to change the subject, tell him something interesting. 'Miss Casey from school is going to Spain to run a café and sell jewellery,' she blurted out.

23

Laddy stopped polishing for a moment. 'Babe Casey is really jumping ship?'

'Do you know her?' she asked.

'Everyone knows Babe, she's a teacher, hangs round with Watches O'Brien.'

'What a funny name.'

'Not at all. He sells watches, whatever kind you want – Rolex, Gucci. You know.'

'Oh,' said Star, who didn't know.

'So poor old Watches has gone to Spain? And the Babe is going after him to set up a little home? That's funny.'

'They're not going to get married, but as good as,' Star explained.

'Yeah, that's for sure, Mrs Watches wouldn't like it if she thought he was getting married.'

'You mean he's married already?' Star was shocked.

'Sure, at least once.' Laddy was unconcerned. He was sitting on the ground beside his bike, head bent over his work.

'Oh, poor Miss Casey. I bet you she doesn't know.'

'No, pet, she knows, she knows very well,' Laddy said, without looking up.

He had called her 'pet', he had never done

that before. Maybe it was because of her lime-green frilly skirt. They had told her at the market that fellows loved skirts that colour. They might have been right.

Laddy looked up at her. 'Believe me, she knows the score about Mrs Watches and the children . . . It's not something you have to tell Babe. Far from it.'

'Children? He has children? He can't go off if he has children.'

'He's gone already.'

'How do you know all this, Laddy?'

'Watches does a bit of business in the pub where Biddy works and Babe comes down there at night to meet him. Then later, they come into a place where I work from time to time, a club sort of place.'

It was all too much for Star to take in. Miss Casey of all people. Her face showed the shock she felt.

Laddy got up from his work. 'I'm getting a beer, will you share it with me?' he asked.

Star nodded, unable to speak.

He brought out a can from the fridge. There were beads of cold water on the outside. He took a swallow and then passed her the can. She drank it nervously and he kissed her on the forehead. Her first kiss and her first alcohol and this terrible news about Miss Casey, all in the same ten minutes.

'Oh, Star, what are we going to do with you? You're much too good for this world.' Laddy laughed fondly at her.

CHAPTER THREE

THERE WAS A GOING away party for Miss Casey at school. Star was in charge of collecting the money for a gift. Some of the girls wanted to get her a watch, but Star said no, definitely not, she couldn't explain why but she knew a watch was wrong. So they bought her a digital camera instead. Miss Casey seemed very pleased.

'Will you be teaching somewhere else, Miss Casey?' the other girls asked.

'Oh very probably, got to keep the wolf from the door,' Miss Casey said.

Star looked at the ground.

At the end of the little ceremony, most of the girls went out into the playground. Miss Casey gathered up all her good luck cards and took down some of her pictures from the classroom wall.

'No card from you, Star?' Miss Casey said to her quietly.

'I didn't have the money to buy one, Miss Casey,' Star lied.

'The other girls gave me home-made cards.'

'I know. Yes.'

'So you are cross with me? You think I should have told them all I was going off to work the beaches in Spain, do you?'

'Why did you tell *me* then?' Star asked with spirit.

'Because you are different to all those other girls, they only think about lip gloss and wrist bands and boy bands. You are interested in people and you care about them. You care about your brother's job, your sister not eating, your father gambling and your other brother ending up in gaol. In fact, there's a way in which you care too much. So I was stupid enough to think you might care about me and what I was doing.'

'But I *do*, Miss Casey.'

'No, you don't, Star, you are sulking and trying to punish me over something. That's not the action of a friend.'

'Am I your friend, Miss Casey?'

'Of course you are. You know that.'

'I think *I'm* a bit of a mess, really.'

'No, you're just kind and want the best for people. It's not always a wise thing. Most people lead sort of messy lives and you can't really change them.'

'And, Miss Casey, can friends say anything to each other?'

'Well, mainly they can. You have friends of your own, don't you, in the class?'

'Not really. Rita a bit, I suppose, but she's not a real friend. They all think I'm a bit dull, you know.'

'Not dull, it's just that you think about things a lot. I often wondered what you were thinking about all the time.'

'I think it's worrying more than thinking, Miss Casey,' Star said. 'I worry about everyone. I want everything to be all right for everyone.'

'Oh, it will never be all right for everyone, believe me, Star. And do you worry about me?'

'Yes, Miss Casey. I worry about you because you're very nice and a great teacher and I see now *why* there were wars and treaties. Once I thought we just had to learn them, now I see why things happened. And I suppose I don't want you to go.'

'But it would be all right if I was going to

teach at another school, not what I am going to do? Is that it?'

'A bit, yes.'

'Star, you are fourteen years of age, you are almost a woman. You are old enough to know that people fall in love and take risks.'

'But he has a wife and children, Miss Casey.'

'Who has?'

'Mr Watches.'

'Boy, you did your homework. How did you know?'

'Laddy Hale told me.'

'And how do you know Laddy Hale?'

'He lives next door.'

'God, this place is a village,' Miss Casey said with a great sigh.

'So I was upset,' Star explained.

'Well, don't be upset,' Miss Casey said, with a tight, hard smile. 'If I were to teach you nothing else in the world except this, remember it. There is no use in God's earth being upset by the things that other people do, only what you do yourself.'

And Miss Casey left the room without a goodbye.

*

Star tried to obey this rule but it was very hard.

How could you not be upset when a horse had fallen and Dad had lost all the holiday money that Mam had been saving for a week in a caravan?

What kind of person would not be upset when Lilly was taken into hospital and they said her eating disorder was very serious, like a form of madness, and that one in four people who had it died from it? Lilly looked awful. She had hair all over her face now and her elbows stuck out like jagged bones.

And Kevin had a horrible girlfriend called Gemma who was a pain in the face and he was nearly always at her place and hardly ever at home.

Michael had left school and he was working for Laddy's father, helping him load plants and deliver them to people's cars in the gardening centre. Star was very worried because he was wearing a black leather jacket that she knew cost the earth. And no matter how many tips he got from customers, they could not have added up to that jacket.

And Laddy had a new girlfriend in a short red skirt with long tanned legs. Her name was

Topper, which Star thought was very silly. Sometimes she stayed the night in number 23. Imagine! In front of Laddy's father and Biddy, she would just come out as cool as anything in the morning with a mug of tea and admire Mr Hale's flowers, and they all thought it was perfectly normal.

And Star's mother seemed to be very tired and had twice fallen in dizzy spells at the supermarket.

And yet Miss Casey had told her that the most important thing in the world was not to worry about other people and get upset. It was getting harder and harder to do.

Star was not happy at school either. The teacher who had replaced Miss Casey for English and History was much too interested in passing exams and not at all interested in telling them why things happened or what the poet felt when he was talking about his lake, island, the sea or whatever. Instead they just had to learn great chunks of things that the teacher had written about imagery. It was very hard and Star soon fell behind.

When she was nearly sixteen she decided that there was no point in staying on at school.

Mam could get her a job in the supermarket, and she would be bringing in some money, which they badly needed. Kevin didn't give anything at home. Lilly had left her job, being sick and everything. Michael was on probation now and had been fired from the garden centre where Mr Hale worked. Her father had been having very bad luck on the horses and as a result owed Certain People a lot of money, so even though he worked like a dog his whole wage packet went straight to the Certain People, not to her mam.

Nobody took much interest in Star leaving school. Nobody except Laddy.

'You're mad to quit now,' he said to her, when she told him her news.

'Why? Didn't you leave school early?' Star asked.

'Not as early as fifteen, and anyway I regret it. I often think that if my mother had been around I would have stayed on and got a career.'

'But you *have* a career,' Star cried. 'You do a bit of this and a bit of that.'

'Star, I help to run a cycling club, I store dodgy things in that shed, I drive even more

33

dodgy things in a big van, I work hours as a barman in one club and as a bouncer in another. Is that a career?'

'It's a lot of careers,' she said, her eyes shining.

'Don't you want to learn more things, know more?' he said.

'Not really. I just want things to be all right for everyone, that's all I want.'

'It's a pretty big wish,' Laddy said.

Lilly was still in hospital and barely knew who Star was. The boys were too busy and Dad was too upset about the people who had lent him money. Only Mam knew about Star's new yellow coat and her yellow and white hat and how she went to work at the bakery section of the supermarket, handing out rolls and scones to people, with little pincers. Only Molly Sullivan saw the way people smiled at her kind, willing daughter who looked so pretty and eager to please. Some day someone would break Star's heart into pieces. She was the kind of girl to trust anyone who said anything nice at all.

At last the hospital were sending Lilly home. Molly and Star were getting her room ready for her. There were only three bedrooms at number 24 Chestnut Street, one for Mam and Dad, one for the boys and one for the girls. But Lilly would need a room of her own now. Kevin was hardly ever in the house but Michael was still around, so where did that leave Star?

She told Laddy about it as she told him everything. Topper didn't seem to be round so much any more. Laddy said he had the perfect solution. He needed someone to keep an eye on things in their shed at night. Michael could have a bed there, and he would set it up straight away.

So before Lilly was back from hospital it had all been done. Laddy had given the boys a tin of white paint each to freshen up all the bedrooms, and he supervised the job. He got Kevin to move all his gear over to Gemma's flat. Kevin didn't like it.

'But how can Star sleep in your old room with all your weight-training stuff and trainers?' Laddy asked.

There was no answer. Kevin complained that Gemma would want a ring on her finger if much more of this went on.

Star looked around her bright, clean, new

room. Laddy had even put up shelves for her in the corner and given her a blue rug for the floor. From the window she could see the garden shed where her brother Michael was now sleeping. The shed that Laddy had told her was full of dodgy things.

Michael now made breakfast for Mr Hale and Laddy in the mornings. Big mugs of tea, just as they liked it, and two pieces of toast each. Star's mam was amazed that Michael would do that in someone else's house when she had never been able to make him do it in his own.

'I wasn't hard enough on him, I suppose,' she told Star.

'But you wouldn't have wanted a row,' Star said, as if it was very clear and simple.

'That's it, Star, I never wanted a row,' her mother said.

Michael didn't want anyone coming into his shed. 'It's the Hales' business, that shed,' he would say, if anyone asked. So Star and her mother had given up. Kevin didn't ask and Lilly didn't care.

One night, Star stood behind her curtain and watched as Michael and Laddy carried what must have been fifty boxes from the shed into a waiting van. Then Michael got into the driver's seat and headed off. Michael, who had no driving licence, driving a van full of stolen goods!

And then when he had gone she saw Laddy sweep out the shed carefully and put the rubbish in a black plastic sack. He went back into the house, leaving the shed door open. This was a chance for Star to see what it was like so she stole downstairs and peeped around the open door.

It was empty of boxes now. All it contained was just Michael's single bed, a red rug on it and a red reading lamp beside it. A coat-stand too where he hung his clothes. Very simple, certainly. Her heart thumping about the danger they must be in, she crept back to her room.

At dawn there was a lot of noise. The bin men were due to collect the rubbish that day. Without thinking, Star went and took Laddy's black rubbish bag from next door and added it to their own bags.

An hour later two police cars arrived. Laddy was being questioned about his movements on the previous night. Over and over he claimed to have been at home in Chestnut Street.

Where was Michael Sullivan?

He said the boy had gone off somewhere on a train.

'Not in a van?' the sergeant asked.

'No, I don't think he has a driving licence.' Laddy looked innocent.

'And your father was asleep, your stepmother was away, so there are no witnesses of where you were last night?'

Star Sullivan stepped forward. 'I was with him all night,' she said in a clear voice.

'And you are . . . ?'

'Star Sullivan, Laddy's next-door neighbour and girlfriend.'

'Where did you spend the night?'

'In the shed, in a single bed with a red rug and a red light.' Star spoke very definitely.

'This is so, Mr Hale?'

'This is so,' said Laddy.

CHAPTER FOUR

AFTER THAT EVERYTHING CHANGED. Star was the centre of a lot of attention in the Sullivan home.

'Did you know she was sleeping with that fellow next door?' Shay asked Molly.

'No idea on God's earth,' Molly said, still shocked by it all.

'Well, it's up to you to make sure she's . . . all right, you know.'

'It's a bit late to be thinking about that now,' Molly said. 'Either she's being sensible or she isn't, and you know Star.'

But apparently they didn't know Star.

Kevin her eldest brother was also shocked. 'Making herself cheap with everyone all over the place,' he said.

'I wouldn't say that,' Molly began.

'What *would* you say, Mam?' Kevin asked.

'Not much,' Molly agreed.

Lilly was astounded. How could someone

who was as old as Laddy and as good-looking have gone for little Star who was fat and foolish? Nice, of course, but boring.

'Men don't always look for brains, you know,' Molly said 'And I'll have you know that Star is far from fat, she's grand-looking.'

Only Michael knew that it wasn't true. When he came back from his trip to hear that he had just missed being put in gaol again, and this time thanks to his little sister, he sat down with the shock.

'She was here in my bed with you?' he said to Laddy.

'Of course she wasn't. She just *said* that.'

'She's very young for you, Laddy.'

'God, Michael, I wasn't near her, she just came out of a clear blue sky and said it, and got us both off the hook. You had dropped me in it, you know that.'

'It's not like Star to think so quickly.'

'I know. She even got rid of the black rubbish bag, gave it to the bin men and all.'

'Well, wouldn't people surprise you?' Michael said, delighted.

He gave Star a very smart mobile phone. As a thank-you present.

'Ah no, really, Michael, thank you, but no. I don't really have anyone to phone.'

'What *would* you like then?'

'I've got everything, Michael, a lovely room of my own and a nice job. I'm fine.'

He looked at her. She meant it.

Laddy also asked her what he could give her to thank her for thinking so quickly. She told him she didn't need anything at all.

He was puzzled by her. Years of odd jobs here and there and time spent in nightclubs had not prepared Laddy for a girl like Star, who truly could not think of any present she might like. Topper would have known, so would Biddy, so would almost everyone Laddy had ever met.

'What would you like best in the world, Star?' he asked.

Star thought hard about the question. 'I suppose I'd like Dad to have one big win that would pay off all that he owes and for him never to gamble again,' she said, after a while.

'But that's not going to happen. If he did have one big win, then he'd think he would have another, and it would just start all over again.'

'He might have learned his lesson,' Star said.

41

'What else would you like?'

'I'd like Lilly to eat properly and not to have her bones sticking out. She doesn't eat *anything*. I try to hide it from Mam.'

'That's not sensible,' Laddy said.

'I know, but I don't want more fights. And then I'd like someone to look after Michael and keep him out of trouble. It's not *much* to ask, but it's kind of hard to organise.' She looked very young and innocent. Her eyes were big and full of hope. Her red-brown hair was shiny.

Laddy stroked her face. 'All right, we'll see what we can do. Give your father one big win, for example,' he said.

'He has no money, you see,' she began.

'I'll lend it to him. Not today, in a couple of weeks. Not a word, right?'

'Not a word,' Star said.

'And we'll see what we can do about Lilly and Michael,' Laddy promised.

They were surprised in number 24 that Star didn't seem to go out with Laddy. Sometimes they asked her.

'Has he dropped you, then, now that he's got what he wanted?' Lilly wondered.

'If he's treating you badly, just tell me,' Kevin said, with a great frown.

'Not going out with your fellow, then?' her father would ask.

'He's a good bit too old for you, Star, you'd be much better off finding someone of your own age,' Molly would say.

Star never said anything. Other people brought it up. Like Biddy, who lived in the Hales' house and everyone assumed was the girlfriend of Laddy's dad.

'You do surprise me,' Biddy said to her one day. 'But then, they always say watch out for the quiet ones. He's a bit of a handful, our Laddy, but he's worth waiting for, they tell me.'

Star tried to look as if Laddy had been well worth waiting for.

Topper, the girl in the short skirts, came round. Star was working in the garden, as she often was. Topper sat on the wall as she talked.

'You didn't take long to move in when I left,' she said.

Star tried to look as if she was someone who was used to moving in quickly.

'He won't be faithful to you, he doesn't know how,' Topper said, in a pleased voice. 'I just thought you should know. I was only going out with him for three weeks when he found someone else.'

'Oh dear,' Star said.

'And when I made a fuss, he said that's the way he was. Has he said that to you?'

'No, no, he hasn't.'

'But you haven't made a fuss yet, have you?'

'No, no, I didn't make any fuss,' Star agreed.

'You will,' said Topper, 'and it will do you no good.'

At the supermarket, Kenny who worked at the fish counter asked her out. Star was about to say no when she realised that maybe Laddy would take more notice of her if he believed her to be the kind of girl who had real dates. So she agreed to go to the pictures with Kenny and then for a Chinese meal.

But none of it mattered to Star, except to tell Laddy. She had a real date. He would have to be impressed.

Laddy said the movie was brilliant. He had seen it on a dodgy DVD and it was first class. He said she should go for prawns and sesame toast at the Chinese restaurant. 'We must make a good impression on this Kenny,' he said.

Star felt tears of rage in her eyes. This was *not* the response she had expected or wanted. What had happened to good old-fashioned jealousy?

Then Laddy remembered something. 'Your father's big bet will be coming up in a week or so. Start talking to him about this trainer. Say you heard about it at work, don't let it get back to me.'

'I wish now I'd never told you about my dad,' Star said. 'I'm starting to worry all over again.'

'No, it will be fine when the time comes. I'll lend him a thousand euro and he'll win a fortune.'

Star nearly fainted. 'A *thousand* euro on top of what he owes! Oh, Laddy, this is terrible.'

'Just keep me well out of it. I'm simply his banker, better that way.'

Star hardly remembered her date with Kenny, except that he was nice but very dull.

She said she couldn't go out with him again as she had family problems, which was very true. She was worried sick about what she and Laddy were planning for her father.

45

He had been interested enough when she spoke about the trainer, said he had two good horses in a race next week. One was called Lone Star, that was the more heavily fancied. Then the day before the race, Laddy told her to tell her father that she had heard in the supermarket that Lone Star was limping, but that Small Screen was home and dry.

'Where do you hear all these things? They never tell me anything like that,' Molly complained.

'That's because, unlike little Star here, you wouldn't bring the news home with you,' Shay said.

'Well, it's not going to be any use to you, Shay, you don't have any money,' Star's mother said. Shay's mouth went into a hard, sad line.

Later that evening Laddy came in to know if he could borrow Shay to help with some furniture that had to be shifted upstairs. Young Michael was off having a driving lesson before his test next week. Laddy's father was out at the pub. Laddy said he would be so grateful and there would be twenty euro in it in case Shay wanted a bet.

Star could see them from her bedroom

window. Arms waving, assurances being given. Life and hope had returned to her father's face again.

He came back holding the twenty-euro note, but Star could see a bulge in his hip pocket where he had the wad of extra notes. Molly, glad to see Shay so happy again, said he could also have the fifty euro she had been saving for a treat.

'No, no, you're all right,' Shay said, gruffly.

'Go on, Shay, take it, then that's a real bet for you,' Molly said, and Shay looked embarrassed and a bit red in the face.

They sat and watched the race next day, Shay, Molly, Lilly and Star. Small Screen was ten to one.

'Imagine! That would be seven hundred euro if you won, Shay!' Molly said.

Star couldn't speak. She knew that it would be 10,700 euro if he won. And that he would owe Laddy Hale 1,000 euro if he lost. She could barely watch, until she heard them cheering.

'What happened to Lone Star?' she asked weakly.

'Your friends at the supermarket weren't wrong, my angel, though how they knew I'll never know. Poor little Lone Star stumbled after a hurdle and went lame. Jockey couldn't get anything out of her after that.'

Star's dad went out for a pint with Laddy to collect his winnings and celebrate. Star watched them with anxious eyes. Had she made a pact with the devil? Laddy *must* have known that Lone Star was going to fall. Was he a fortune-teller? Could he tell the future? Or did he know something about the race that he should not have known?

Whatever the reason, did it now mean that her father was more addicted than ever to the horses? Star bit her lip and said nothing while her mother and sister planned how they would all ideally spend the 700 euro that they believed were the winnings.

Then her father came home with what seemed like a fistful of money.

'Your mother gets five hundred, that was her investment, so that's fair,' he began. They looked at him open-mouthed. 'And one hundred each for Star and Lilly. That's it, fair and square.' He handed it out.

'But what about you, Daddy? It was your bet.' Star was hardly able to get the words out.

'No, I had a good race, and a good lesson. I realised how nearly I had put it all on Lone Star, how very, very nearly. *All* that huge amount of money.'

'It was only seventy euro in the end, Shay, it wasn't the biggest bet you ever had,' Molly said.

'Enjoy your winnings, girls,' he said, and went to watch a sitcom.

'Whatever they say or write about it,' Molly said eventually, 'there's no way to understand men. No way at all.'

Star got herself a new hairstyle and bought a new outfit with her 100 euro. The dress was copper-coloured, just like her hair, with a big cream collar. It was oddly old-fashioned but it suited her perfectly. The girl in the shop said it made her look like someone in a painting. Even Lilly, who normally never said anything nice, praised it.

Laddy was full of admiration. 'Is that to dazzle Kenny the Fish?' he asked.

'Who?' Star said.

'You know, the guy who took you for the Chinese meal,' Laddy said.

He had remembered. That was good. 'No, no,

not at all, just spending my father's winnings before he changes his mind about them and wants them back for the three-thirty somewhere tomorrow.'

'He won't do that,' Laddy said.

'How do you know?'

'I told him how the race was fixed, I told him how I knew. I told him how you all worried about him, laid it on a bit thick, but it worked. He's cured. So say, "Thank you, Laddy," and give me a kiss.'

'Thank you, Laddy.' Star closed her eyes and held her face near his. Laddy kissed her. She opened her mouth slightly like people at school had said you should do, but he didn't put his tongue into her mouth so she closed it again. Eventually Laddy pulled away from her and looked at her.

'You are one lovely girl, Star Sullivan,' he said. 'One day you're going to make a man very, very, very happy.'

'One day?' she said, disappointed.

'Well, not yet, surely?' he laughed. 'You're not even seventeen. You have the world to see, the Kenny the Fishes to go out with, lands to visit, things to do, all before you settle down.'

To Star it all seemed a great waste of time. She was so ready to settle down. Now. This minute.

CHAPTER FIVE

EVEN THOUGH SHE HAD come home from hospital, Lilly still had to go to the special clinic there twice a week and keep a food diary. The doctor said she was getting on fine.

Michael had been in no trouble lately that anyone had heard of.

Kevin and Gemma announced that they were getting married in a year and a half's time. When they had saved for a proper reception.

Molly was doing fewer shifts at the super-market. She had had her veins injected and had been told to walk long distances every day. On one of her long walks she saw Laddy Hale with his arm around a pretty little blonde. Every few yards they stopped to kiss each other.

Molly didn't intend to tell Star this news. The child was barely seventeen now and still hung around the small front garden of 24 Chestnut Street in the hopes of meeting the handsome boy next door.

Star had developed an interest in gardening so that she had an excuse to talk to Mr Hale about plants. He brought her nice winter pansies and ornamental cabbages, as well as little heathers and dwarf azaleas and a bag full of the right soil to plant them in.

Sometimes he gave her sweet-smelling plants like night-scented stock, which she planted for poor blind Miss Mack at number 3.

It was easy to talk to Mr Hale but he was quite hopeless if she tried to bring the conversation around to Laddy. He seemed to know nothing about his own son. Not a thing about what he was like as a child, or who his friends were, or if he missed his mother when she went away. Mr Hale just shrugged helplessly about it all.

'And suppose she came back, you know, Laddy's mother? Would you all like that?'

'I don't suppose Biddy would like it,' he said, after some thought.

'No, but I mean you and Laddy?'

'Well, I don't know, it would be interesting to know where she had been, what she was doing, I suppose. That's all.'

'But wouldn't you have liked her to stay?' Star persisted.

'No one would want someone to stay if they wanted to be off somewhere else,' he replied, as if that was obvious.

Star felt very foolish indeed.

She wished she had a friend, someone to talk to, but Rita, who had been her pal in a way at school, had gone to work as a travel rep in the Canary Islands, and Miss Casey was still in Spain with the man called Watches, and Nessa, who lived a few doors down Chestnut Street, was always busy and never had time to talk to Star. Miss Mack was so old that she wouldn't be much help.

There was nobody at work, because all the other girls said she was mad not to fancy Kenny, who now ran not only the whole fish section, but a lot of the deli as well. He was going onwards and upwards and was real management material. Star was crazy to tell him that she didn't really want to go out with him again in case it was leading him on.

Wouldn't it be great to have someone you could talk to about everything? Isn't that what everyone wanted? Or was it only in movies and magazines that people had those kind of friends? Someone who would sit and listen about Laddy, and tell her that he didn't *really* care about the stream of young, barely dressed women who paraded in and out of number 23. A friend who would tell her that yes, OK, he might have been moving some stolen goods that night she had lied for him, but basically he wasn't a criminal. And even though he did know someone who knew someone who had fixed a horse race, it didn't mean that he moved with the underworld all the time.

A friend who would tell Star what to wear, how to act in a way that would make Laddy love her now, just like she loved him.

Her mother tried to be that friend but it was useless. Nobody confides properly in a mother. Molly had asked Star many times whether she was being sensible. She meant, was she using condoms or taking the pill. Star couldn't explain that she had not had sex with Laddy, or indeed with anyone, because she had told everyone that she and Laddy had spent the night together in the single bed under the red rug. In fact Star almost believed that they had.

Lilly looked on Star with more respect these days, too. Normally she thought of Star as someone who didn't tell tales about her hiding food. Lilly was well enough to work now, and she sold clothes in a smart boutique. Laddy next door had helped her get the job because he knew someone. He said she had great style, and that if she could eat a bit more to get some curves and a nice bottom she'd do great, and maybe even get discovered. The boutique owner asked Lilly to wear long-sleeved blouses so that nobody could see her thin, bony arms and the great sockets in her shoulders. All Lilly's time at the clinic was helping her, and nobody had heard the sound of her vomiting in the night, not for a long time now, and she didn't hide food all over the house as she once used to.

Michael had a job too. In a video shop where he worked very odd hours. Sometimes he was out all night. When asked about it, Michael just shrugged. A lot of people were shift workers, he said, and they needed to rent a couple of movies at any time of the day or night. No one else in the family thought it was odd, so Star said nothing. But she worried about Michael as she worried about everything. She couldn't ask Laddy, as it would sound like just what she was, a nagging little sister.

Laddy didn't seem to have anyone particular at the moment. Between girlfriends, maybe. But he wasn't in the garden as much as he used to be. Star watered the Hales' mixed borders as well as their own, and she did a little weeding as well. Laddy might not notice, but his father would and might praise her across the fence.

One afternoon, when she was working in the Hales' garden, Star looked up at the house and saw Laddy pulling the curtains closed in the front bedroom. That was odd. She hadn't seen him go in with any new girlfriend. And anyway he slept at the back of the house. As she looked she caught his eye. Quickly, Star lowered her eyes and finished weeding the flower bed. The curtains in Laddy's father's room were still drawn when she stood up and walked back home.

By the time Owen Hale came back from the garden centre, Biddy had gone off to her job at the bar. His son Laddy had driven off in a van to this or that. And his neighbour Star Sullivan was sitting on the little wooden seat, staring straight ahead. Not able to believe what she knew was true. Not wanting to think about it but unable to get it out of her mind.

Next day at the supermarket, one of the women customers suddenly broke down. She was about fifty. She started to cry and couldn't stop. Then she began to hit out at things and knock them down from the shelves. All the time she was calling out: 'No, Declan, no, don't go away, Declan, stay with me and love me, Declan, like you used to.' Over and over again.

People watched, shocked, and all of them powerless to do anything in the face of such grief. All except Star Sullivan who went over and guided the woman to a chair. Then she removed from her hand the folded umbrella that was doing all the damage and replaced it with a paper cup of very sweet tea. She knelt beside the woman who was still crying out in despair and spoke to her gently.

As people watched in disbelief, Star Sullivan murmured and soothed. 'He's not really gone away, he *does* love you, he only *thinks* he doesn't. It will all be all right. It will all be fine. Sip your tea now. Slowly. He hasn't gone away really, just for now . . .'

And Kenny, who ran the fish and deli counters, held the security men back, and told the other customers that the show was over. By the time he had got the staff nurse to the scene, Star had it all under control and had used the woman's mobile phone to call one of her daughters.

As she meekly left the supermarket, the woman looked drained and empty, as if all the life had been sucked out of her.

Everyone congratulated Star.

'I did nothing,' Star said. 'Nothing, except tell her lies.'

'You stopped her breaking up the shop,' Kenny said with admiration.

'That's not important,' Star said. 'Declan's not coming back to her, is he? He doesn't love her like he once did.'

'Do you know them?' Kenny asked.

'No, I don't, but you heard her, didn't you, and you saw her daughter? She says that he's not coming back.'

And from where she sat at the till Molly looked on and worried about her youngest child.

*

That evening Owen Hale called in at number 24.

'It's Biddy's birthday on Saturday. Don't ask how old she is or she'll go mad, but I thought we'd have a few people in for a barbecue in the afternoon, and you're all very welcome.'

In the old days Shay Sullivan would have been busy choosing winners and standing in a booth at the bookies, watching all his money disappear. In the old days Molly would have been too tired to go out, Lilly would have been afraid to go anywhere where there might be food, Kevin wouldn't have wanted to be in the same space as his father, and Michael would have said he hated neighbours and couldn't be bothered.

But these were not the old days any more so the Sullivans said they would love to come. Star said nothing. Molly noticed, but knew better than to ask a direct question.

'What will you wear, Star?' she asked later.

'Wear? When?'

'To the barbecue next door, on Saturday,' her mother said.

'Oh, I'm not going. I've got a date that afternoon. With Kenny.'

'You are? When did he ask you?'

'I'm asking him. Tomorrow,' Star said.

Kenny said that he would be delighted to go on a picnic with Star. He would bring a bottle of wine and some crab claws and a dipping sauce. He would pick her up at three, which was when the barbecue next door was due to start.

Star wore a blue cotton dress with a pattern of little white flowers. She had a big copper-coloured belt that matched her hair exactly. Even Lilly, not known for compliments, said she thought Star looked terrific.

'He must be special, this Kenny,' she said.

'He's a nice fellow,' Star shrugged.

'More than nice if you're bringing him home to meet the family *and* missing a barbecue at Lovely Laddy's place,' Lilly said.

'I'm not bringing him to meet the family. Mam knows him already from work.'

'You can't fool me,' Lilly said.

Lilly said she was bringing a friend to the party. His name was Nick, he was a journalist, and no mention of Lilly's time in hospital was to be mentioned by anyone, was that understood?

Gemma and Kevin would be there, and Michael had been spending the morning

61

hammering and getting the barbecue pit ready.

Various neighbours from Chestnut Street were coming. Even Miss Mack was being helped across because she had said she loved sausages cooked in the open air better than any other food on earth. Mrs Ryan in number 14, who had an 'understanding' with the builder next door in number 15, had said she would come. Lillian, the hairdresser in number 5, wouldn't be able to come because she was busy, but she had been over in the morning to invite Biddy for a free hairdo as a birthday present. Bucket Maguire, who cleaned windows and operated from number 11, gave the downstairs windows of the Hale household a quick shine and polish in honour of the day.

While Biddy was having her hair done, the men made a big sign and hung it out the window: *Happy Birthday, Biddy*.

Normally it would have been the kind of gathering that Star Sullivan would have loved with all her heart. The sight of neighbours getting together to celebrate a birthday. But this was not normal, far from it. She hadn't been able to look at Laddy since she had seen him drawing the curtains that day. His own father's girlfriend! The woman living in the same house as him, like his stepmother! It was disgusting. And even if Biddy was nearer to Laddy's age than to Owen's, *that* didn't change anything.

When Kenny arrived, Shay Sullivan offered him a beer.

'No, thank you, Mr Sullivan, I'm driving.' Kenny was reliable, responsible.

Just then Laddy Hale, who had never been reliable or responsible in his life, came in to borrow a couple of chairs.

'Hey, Star, don't you look just gorgeous!' he said.

'Thank you, Laddy.' Her voice was flat.

Laddy looked at Kenny. Just looked him up and down.

'Hi, I'm Kenny.' The smile was open and honest.

Laddy didn't smile. 'Sure you are,' he said. 'Kenny the Fish, isn't it?'

'I beg your pardon?'

'And so you *should* beg my pardon, taking the attention of the best-looking girl in Chestnut Street.'

'Let's go now, Kenny,' Star begged.

'But you *can't* go. The party hasn't started yet. Come on, Kenny, use your influence with her, tell her she can't leave now.'

Kenny looked helpless. 'Well, if you'd like to stay for a bit, Star, we're in no hurry. I didn't know there was going to be a party to drag you away from.'

'Star knew, she's known for two weeks,' Laddy said.

'So what about –?' Kenny began, eager to please, to be polite.

'What about leaving now, Kenny?' Star said, in a voice so unlike her usual tones that everyone looked up. And they went out to the car, carrying her picnic basket and looking just like a picture.

Laddy stood at the gate, holding the two chairs, and watched them drive off. Kenny could see him in the driving mirror, still watching.

'That's the boy next door, then,' he said eventually.

'Laddy Hale,' Star said.

'Yes, well, he didn't introduce himself. Nice guy, is he?'

'Not really.' Star spoke slowly. 'No, not a nice guy, unreliable as anything.'

'But very keen on you,' Kenny said.

Star laughed aloud. 'If only you knew! Not keen on me at all. Hardly notices me in fact, but very keen on himself and the effect he has on people. That's Laddy for you!'

'Sorry to disagree with you, Star, but he hated seeing you come away with me. Hated it, I tell you.'

'Good,' said Star, pleased, and settled back in her seat.

CHAPTER SIX

THE PICNIC HAD SEEMED endless. Star thought that it would never be time to go home.

Kenny had been so nice. He asked nothing more about Laddy, instead he talked about the supermarket and how wonderful Star had been with the disturbed customer. Even the General Manager had heard, Kenny reported back. Much praise had been directed towards Miss Sullivan in bakery and confectionery. If Star wanted to move on within the supermarket, or to go on a training course, she would find the management very willing to say yes.

Kenny seemed to love the whole supermarket world and was always absorbed in all its comings and goings. Star was more interested in the woman who had had a breakdown. Her family had written to the supermarket, saying how grateful they were for the way it had all been handled.

'That's all down to you, Star,' Kenny had said proudly, over and over.

He didn't know where the woman lived or anything about the man Declan who didn't love her any more. The woman's daughters were in their thirties and well heeled, he said, they had offered compensation for the smashed goods but it had been refused. The supermarket had behaved well, everyone had behaved well. The poor woman was on some medication, he said, which she hadn't taken that day. It wasn't her fault. It was good to be in a situation where everyone had done the right thing.

'Declan didn't,' Star said. 'Declan promised that he would love her always, but he stopped loving her, that's what it was all about.'

Kenny looked troubled by this. Star was reliving the woman's agony too much. She should be glad that, thanks to her own quick thinking, it had all been tidied away.

He produced a folding table and two little chairs. He told her he had bought them at a staff discount in the leisure section of the super-market when Star had first suggested a picnic. He had even brought a checked tablecloth and a little vase with one flower in it.

They ate their picnic meal together, the crab claws he had brought, the dainty tomato sandwiches and some little currant buns she had baked. They sipped their wine and drank the flask of coffee Star had made.

Kenny searched for more subjects to entertain her but she was miles away. Star tried to listen and be interested but they seemed to be talking round in circles.

'I hope your father likes me,' he said suddenly.

'Why wouldn't he like you?'

'Well, I hope to be coming round to 24 Chestnut Street quite often, taking his beautiful daughter out. It would be better if he liked me. You say he works in a hotel kitchen. Is he a chef?'

'No, he's just a helper really. He used to have a big gambling problem, you see, but he got over it.'

'He must be a strong man, then.'

'Not really, someone sort of helped him. Now he's much more interested in the family, not the horses, so it's a lot better.'

'Does he like your sister's boyfriend, do you think?'

'Lilly? Oh, I don't think that Nick is a boyfriend, I think he's only a journalist,' Star said.

Kenny laughed. 'He could be both, you know, there isn't a law against it.'

He looked so nice and normal when he laughed she felt a wave of anger that she couldn't like him more.

'You're so good, Kenny,' she said, laying her hand on his on the tablecloth. 'You deserve someone much better than me.'

'There *is* no one better than you,' he said, and he meant it. 'Star, you are the very, very best person I have ever met. I *love* being in your company, I just hope you like me, that's all.'

'I *do* like you, Kenny. It's just that . . . it's just that . . .' Her voice trailed away.

'It's just that you are too young to get involved with anyone yet, is that it?' His face was full of hope.

'Not really,' she began.

'No, don't say anything. I *know*. You are very young, but I'll wait, Star, I won't put pressure on you, I'll look out for you at work, but I won't nag at you to come out with me. I didn't before,

69

remember, it's only that you suggested this picnic and I wondered . . . I hoped . . .'

Star said nothing.

'I think you are wonderful,' he said simply.

'You don't know. You don't know anything.'

'No, but you'll tell me what you want me to know.'

'I can't, Kenny, it's too complicated. Everyone thinks I've slept with Laddy. That's just for starters.'

'Why do they think that?' He was calm.

'Because I *said* that I did, in order to cover up for him and my brother who were moving stolen goods.'

'And why did you say that, Star?'

'It seemed the easiest thing to do, and Laddy was very pleased with me.'

'I bet he was,' Kenny said.

'And he was very nice to me for a while afterwards, but then he kept bringing in lots of girlfriends, parading them past me. And it's very hard, you see, very upsetting.'

'Because you like him?'

'I don't like him at all, that's the point. I *really* don't like him, specially now. Now that he's sleeping with his stepmother.'

'*What?*'

'Well, Biddy who lives with Laddy's father, she's about thirty. Yes, that's what she must be today, I didn't think. Laddy's twenty-two, and his father is about fifty. It's so sick and awful. It shouldn't have happened between them. It's so wrong.' She spoke fast now, just like the woman in the supermarket, in a great wail.

'But you don't *know* if any of this is true. Maybe it's a mistake,' Kenny said.

'I do know it's true.'

'But he couldn't be having all that party for her, together with his father, if he had . . . if they . . . you know.'

'They did, believe me, they did.'

'Listen, you say you don't like him, so what does it matter? What does he matter? Put him out of your mind.'

'I can't, I really can't. You see, all day and all night I don't think of anything or anyone else. Nothing but Laddy. It's driving me mad.'

'You *love* him!' Kenny was astonished.

'I have no idea what love is any more, but all I can tell you is that I think about him night and day and wish that I *had* gone to bed with him in the big shed like I said I did. Then he might not find it so easy to ignore me and hurt me so much.'

'Oh poor little Star,' Kenny said. 'You poor, lovely thing.'

And she laid her head on his shoulder while he patted her beautiful, shiny hair and her shaking shoulders under the blue and white dress as she sobbed her heart out to him.

Nobody forgot Biddy's thirtieth birthday. That was the day that a friend of Shay Sullivan's rang him and told him about a greyhound that could not lose. Real and serious money could be made. Anyone who had access to 5,000 euro or more would be home and dry. Shay had access. But it would mean getting it back from Laddy that same day. The day of the big birthday party next door. Not good timing, not an easy thing to do, especially since Shay had assured Laddy that he would never gamble again. And had it not been for the certainty of this greyhound, he never would have wanted to.

He thought it all through slowly and came to a decision. It wasn't worth all the hassle of trying to lay his hands on the cash. What was it in the end except either more or less money? He had enough other things going well for him in life.

Molly wasn't working double shifts in the supermarket any more, she was well and happy. Often she would sit with her legs up on a footstool, reading little bits about famous people out of the papers.

His eldest son Kevin was not only speaking to him again, but had come to work in the same hotel as Shay. Together they were planning to set up a health-food snack bar in the leisure centre. The boy was marrying that nice Gemma next year. All was good on that front.

Lilly was cured of her terrible eating problems and she now had a nice young man who was a journalist. He had even arranged for her to do some fashion shoots once she had put on a little more weight.

Michael hadn't been in any kind of trouble for months now. He had a great job as a driver, which paid very well.

Little Star had this Kenny from the supermarket completely mad about her, according to Molly. She didn't hang around the garden any more hoping to catch a glimpse of Laddy.

And suppose he *did* have a big win? What

would it mean? That he would have 40,000 euro safe in Laddy Hale's hands rather than 9,000 euro, which he already had. What would he buy? Nothing, really. The days were gone when he would put it all on another animal before sunset. Better leave his nest egg, don't disturb things. It was safe where it was.

Well, he supposed it was safe. Shay remembered that Laddy was hardly a pillar of the law. But the boy would never have run off with Shay's winnings. He wouldn't do that, surely? Of course he *had* slept with Star, which made Shay a little uneasy. She was so young and trusting, but then, young girls nowadays? There was no telling them. And from all accounts Star had been willing, very willing.

But somehow the faintly uneasy feeling about Laddy persisted all afternoon, and even as Shay stood beside him, turning lamb chops, bacon and sausages on the barbecue, he felt sudden doubts about the boy.

'There's a sure thing at Harold's Cross tonight,' he said eventually.

Laddy smiled at him lazily. 'Ah, you're over all that sort of stuff Shay,' he said.

'It never quite goes away,' Shay said.

'So?' Laddy asked.

'So if I were to ask you for my money, would you have it?' Shay asked.

'Sorry?' Laddy was puzzled.

'You heard me, Laddy, if I wanted my money that you are minding for me, would you have it?'

'Well, what do *you* think? Do you think I still have it, or do you think that I spent it or stole it or what?' Laddy was angry now. Blustering, Shay thought.

'No, of course not, I just wondered, like . . . Do you have it in the house?'

'Do you want it for tonight? To throw it all on a dog, is that what you're saying?'

'No, I'm saying *suppose* I did want it, how soon could I have it?'

'Monday morning,' Laddy said coldly.

'But not now?'

'Monday morning.' Laddy's face was hard. 'Do you want it then, or not?'

'No, I told you, it's only a matter of asking you about it. What's the point of you keeping it in cash for me if I can't get it whenever I want it?'

'Like a couple of hours before the greyhounds

come out of the trap at Harold's Cross? Oh yeah?' Laddy said scornfully.

'You've got me wrong,' Shay began.

'Yes, I see I must have,' Laddy said, and the sunshine seemed to go out of the day.

Laddy was talking to Molly. 'Is Star going out with Kenny the Fish seriously?'

'Don't call him that, Laddy, he's a nice boy.'

'Not an answer, Molly.'

'The answer is that Star doesn't tell me her business. She didn't tell me she was involved with *you* back then.'

'Back when?'

'Come on, Laddy, you know, back when you and she slept together in the shed.'

'No matter what she said, we didn't, as it happens. She's too young. Still is.'

'So why did she say it, then?' Molly was confused.

'Think, Molly,' he said.

But that left her more confused than ever.

Nick was enjoying the party. 'Tell me more about the big guy in the T-shirt serving the food, I've seen him somewhere.'

'Everyone's seen him somewhere,' Lilly explained. 'That's Laddy Hale, he works in clubs and bars around the place.'

'That's it. I saw him last week, at this big charity thing I was telling you about. One of the VIPs was pissed as a fart and that guy got him out of the place so quick. Told the fellow there were bottles of single malt in a room at the back and then frogmarched him into a taxi. He was home before he realised it. They all thought your man there was great.'

'He had a fling with my sister, Star, once,' Lilly said. If Laddy was cool, she thought, then why not be part of it all?

'Star? Never! She's much too young for him and sort of . . . you know.'

'I know,' Lilly shrugged, 'but it happened.'

Gemma and Kevin told Laddy and his father that when they were married they would have a built-in barbecue in the garden just like the Hales'. It was a real feature and they hoped they would entertain a fair bit once they had their own house.

'Why don't you and Biddy get married?' Gemma asked Owen Hale, in a way that she might not have done, had she not drunk three glasses of wine on a hot day.

'Marry Biddy? Go on out of that, she's years too young for me. Anyway I'd say Biddy will be moving on soon, to the next bit of her life,' Laddy's father said in his easygoing way.

Gemma was shocked. 'But what about love, Mr Hale?'

'Oh, love comes and goes, you'll find that out later. Comes and goes.'

Gemma had to sit down and have two glasses of water to get over this. As an engaged person she did *not* want to believe that love came and went. She preferred to think it lasted for ever.

Michael got a call on his mobile phone and as a result he went home quickly and packed an overnight bag. Very quietly he joined Laddy at the barbecue.

'Can I have the keys to your van? Now, Laddy, please,' he said, his tone urgent.

'Nope. Sorry,' Laddy said.

'You don't understand, I've just had a call . . . I have to – I have to be out of here. Sharpish.'

'Not in my van.' Laddy was smiling at Lillian

the hairdresser and Molly as he heaped their plates.

'I *need* it, Laddy.'

'There's a bus service up on the main road,' Laddy said.

'Why? Why won't you help me?'

'One too many times, Michael, I've rescued you just that once too often. If I were you, I'd get off now quick. I see you've packed your bag.' He turned away.

'Laddy, you're in this as much as I am . . .' Michael was desperate.

'I think you'll find I'm not. Go now, Michael, if you've any sense.'

And Michael realised there would be no van, no hope, no rescuing this time.

'Why did you do it in the past if you won't do it now?'

'If you hurried, you know, you'd be well away before they get here.'

Laddy went on serving the salad with two big plastic serving spoons.

When Kenny brought Star home, her face was still stained with crying. She was very apologetic.

'I'll just creep upstairs to bed, they're all still next door,' she said.

'No, I think you should join the party, otherwise you'll only lie there thinking about it,' Kenny said.

'No, I couldn't go, I look so terrible.'

'I'll wash your face for you,' he said.

'Why are you so nice to me?'

'Because I love you, Star, and I want you to be happy.'

'Even though . . . ?' she began.

'Even though,' he finished for her.

Just as Star slipped into the Hales' garden, Biddy began to make a little speech. She wanted to thank everyone for being so kind to her and giving her such a great party. It was marking a big change in her life. She was heading off to see the world, she said. She had been very happy during her time in Chestnut Street and had made many new friends but now it was time for a middle-aged woman of thirty to move on. Owen and Laddy had arranged this as a going-away party, as well as a birthday, and she was very touched. She would be leaving tomorrow before anyone was up, but she would never forget the people who had turned up here today.

'We'll be gone by eight o'clock at the latest,' she said.

Star held onto a chair. This woman must be taking Laddy with her, her own boyfriend's son. She was standing there telling everyone that she and Laddy were leaving next day. Going off together, out of Star's life for ever.

Star felt the ground first slide away from her and then rush up to meet her. There was a roaring noise in her ears and everything went black.

CHAPTER SEVEN

IT WAS LADDY WHO saw her fall and ran towards her. He carried her into her own house, away from the eyes of the neighbours. Molly made her a cup of sweet tea which brought the colour back to her cheeks.

'Why are you going away?' Star said, as soon as she could speak.

'I'm not going away, it's Biddy who's going, she's off to the Far East with two friends.'

'And not you?'

'Oh, I'm brave all right, but not brave enough to go to Cambodia with those three.'

'But aren't you upset she's going? Isn't your father upset?'

'People go when they want to go, Star, that's the way things are.'

What kind of men were these Hales who would let women walk in and out of their lives?

She turned away her head from him in

disgust. 'You know exactly why she's going,' she said.

'Yes, she and her friends want to travel.'

'No, it's because you and she had an affair.'

'Please, Star, please. You're talking rubbish.'

'No, I'm not, I know what I saw.'

He looked at her with anger. 'You *used* to know a lot, Star, you knew when to keep quiet about things and when to say something helpful. You were a great little mate altogether. Now you've become very odd.'

'That's all you wanted me for, as a helpful little liar next door to cover up your tracks, Laddy Hale. Well, I'm not doing it any more.'

'Star, don't get upset,' her mother begged.

'Mam, go back to the party, please, I'm fine. Go back and sing "For She's a Jolly Good Fellow" for Biddy and everyone like her. I want to talk to Laddy about something.'

'No way, I haven't a notion of talking to you about *anything*, Star Sullivan. You're as sweet as pie, but all the time you're ruining people's lives for them, and dragging other people in to help you. Well, I've helped you for the last time, believe me.'

And he was gone.

Molly looked after him as the door banged behind him. 'In the name of God, Star, what was all that about?' she asked.

'I don't know,' Star said. 'I don't know what he means.'

Biddy left the following morning, just as she said. From behind the curtain in her bedroom Star saw her waving cheerfully at Owen Hale and his son Laddy as she got into a taxi.

All that day there was an air of unease at the Sullivan house. Mainly the family were worried about Star. The bruise where she had hit her head in falling was purple and yellow. Her eyes were dead.

Lilly said that her Nick had told her that Laddy was quite a hero in some club, which she thought would please Star, but it went down like a lead balloon.

Nobody had seen Michael anywhere around since quite early on at the party. Star, who always seemed to know where he was, just shrugged her shoulders. Shay said he didn't feel like going over to ask Owen and Laddy where the boy was. That he had had some words with Laddy the previous day that had been misunderstood. And Molly, who was usually so eager to help any neighbours, said that it mightn't be a good idea to go and help the Hales to tidy up after the barbecue.

Star said nothing at all, just stared in front of her.

At about midday Kenny called by to deliver them the Sunday papers. He was horrified at the sight of Star's face.

'What happened yesterday?' he cried.

'It was *my* fault,' Star began. 'I shouldn't have gone to the party, I should have left well alone. I insisted on going, and then there was a misunderstanding.'

'He did this to you?' Kenny was horrified.

'No, no . . . of course not,' she said, but her voice was shaky and weak.

Kenny thought she was protecting Laddy. The man she still loved in spite of everything.

'He's not getting away with this,' Kenny shouted, and ran next door. Before anyone could stop him he had grabbed Laddy, who was cleaning the barbecue, and started to pummel him.

It took Laddy about thirty seconds to recover from the shock, shake himself free, and land

Kenny a blow that knocked him down. By this time people had arrived from everywhere. Owen Hale was out of his house, Shay was over the hedge, Molly and Star were calling out for them to stop.

Laddy wiped the blood from around his mouth and looked over at Star. 'Well done, kid,' he said. 'There you go again, upsetting everyone's lives with your big innocent eyes.'

'I didn't say anything, I didn't . . .'

'Of course you didn't, Star,' he said, got into his white van and drove away, leaving everyone else to cope with Kenny and to try to work out what had happened.

On Monday Star wasn't well enough to go to work at the supermarket. When Molly came home, she reported that Kenny hadn't been in either.

Shay was barely installed in the kitchen of his hotel when he got a message that someone wanted to see him at the front office.

It was Laddy, carrying a parcel.

'Your money, Shay,' Laddy said in a cold voice. 'I think you'll find it all there, safe and sound.'

'Now listen here, Laddy, I never meant –'

'Yes, you did.'

'If I gave offence, I'm really very sorry.'

'You gave offence, certainly.'

'Will you accept my apology then?'

Laddy shrugged. 'If it makes you feel better.'

'And, Laddy, do you have any idea where Michael is? He hasn't been home.'

'No idea. Sorry.'

'But you *must* know. He works with you.'

'No, he doesn't, Shay, he works for himself.'

'But he *lives* with you.'

'He has a bed in our shed, yes, when he wants to stay there.'

Poor Shay looked bewildered. There seemed to be no answers.

'And, Laddy, again, I'm sorry, we're all sorry about that business yesterday morning. The young fellow from the supermarket, he got the wrong end of the stick.'

'Yes, he did,' Laddy agreed.

There was a silence.

'You're very good to bring this money to me. I don't suppose you'd like to go on holding it for me?'

'No I wouldn't, as it happens.'

'And what would you suggest I do with it, like, put it in the post office or what?'

'I have no idea, and really I couldn't care less,' Laddy said, turned and was gone.

Lilly's Nick, who was turning out to be more of a boyfriend than a journalist, came to supper on Monday evening. He brought a big chocolate cake and cut a slice for everyone. To Star's amazement, Lilly ate a sliver like a normal person. And she didn't disappear to the bathroom to be sick either.

Lilly looked so well these days. The boutique where she worked was having a fashion show. Lilly was going to model three items. Nick was making sure that one of these would get into his paper.

He noticed that the Sullivan family seemed a bit subdued.

'Where's Michael?' he asked.

Michael would liven things up, he was not one for long silences. It had been the wrong question to ask, apparently. Nobody knew where he was and everyone seemed to be blaming someone else. Nick gave up in despair. Sometimes you just couldn't get families right.

*

Star picked up the phone. Michael was on the other end.

'Don't say my name, pretend it's someone else, that fellow from the supermarket or something.' He sounded anxious.

'Oh, hi, Kenny,' Star said. Her mother looked up sharply but nobody else took much notice as Star took the phone upstairs.

'Where are you, Michael, what *is* it?' she whispered to him.

'Star, have you any money, any money at all?'

'No, of course I haven't any real money. I've about sixty euro. Would that do?'

'Listen to me carefully. Laddy is holding some money for Dad, I know he is. Can you get it from him, tell him the rainy day has arrived.'

'Tell him *what* has arrived?'

'You know the way people say they are saving for a rainy day? Well, it's here, it doesn't get much rainier than this. I'm in awful trouble, Star. I have to have the money tonight.'

'I'm not speaking to Laddy, ring him yourself.'

'This is not the time for games.'

'It's not games, let me tell you. *You* talk to him.'

'He won't talk to me,' Michael admitted.

'That makes two of us, then.'

'This isn't a joke, I *have* to have this money.'

'Ask Dad then.'

'I can't *do* that, Star, it's some kind of a secret. I'm not even meant to know about it. It was something you asked Laddy to do way back, to make Dad give up gambling, and Laddy did it, and he's holding some money Dad won. So the money's there, and if you could just tell him that it was for you, Laddy would certainly give it to you. He has a soft spot for you, you know he has.'

'Not any more he doesn't,' Star said and hung up.

'How was Kenny?' Molly asked.

'Kenny?' Star looked at her blankly.

'You were just talking to him,' Molly reminded her.

'Oh yes. That's right. I was.'

'So is he OK?'

'He's the same as always,' Star said.

*

Star met Kenny next day when they both returned to work. He had a black eye and a bruise on his chin. Star had a cut and a bruise on her forehead. She pulled her white bakery hat low over her face and tried not to meet anyone's eye as she served them scones or croissants with her pincers. So she didn't recognise her brother Michael until he hissed at her, 'Star, talk to me.'

'God, I didn't see you, Michael, you look *terrible*! What happened to you?'

'What happened to me is that my sister hung up on me yesterday and I'm in deep, deep trouble.'

'What kind of trouble?'

'Well, these guys I know . . . half know . . . met, anyway . . . They took my van. And now the fellows who own the van want to know where it is.'

'And can't you tell them that the other people stole it?'

'Not really, you see, I wasn't meant to have it out the night it disappeared.'

'But what about the insurance?'

'Wake up, Star, these kind of people don't have insurance.'

91

'Michael, I can't do anything for you, I don't *have* anything. It's Tuesday today, I get paid again on Friday. Would that be any help?'

'By Friday I'll have two broken legs.'

'*No!*'

'Yes. Star, can't you speak to Laddy?'

'I told you, there was awful trouble at the party, you missed it all. Biddy left Mr Hale, and Kenny hit Laddy, and he hit Kenny back, and I fainted and got this.' She showed him her bruised face.

'God, Star, are you serious?'

'Yes, it couldn't have been more horrible.'

'And Kenny?'

'He's got an awful bruise, worse than mine. I haven't talked to *him* either.'

'And why did he hit Laddy?'

'A misunderstanding. He thought Laddy had hit me.'

Michael looked thoughtful. 'Where does he work, this Kenny?'

'Over that way, the fish and deli counters. You're not going to go and hit him too, are you?'

'No, why would I do that?'

'I don't know why anyone does anything,' Star said.

*

At her lunch break she decided to face Kenny and went over to his counter.

'He's gone home,' someone said.

'He's not feeling worse, is he?' Star asked.

The others looked with interest at her face. Could she and Kenny really have had a violent punch-up? Watch the quiet ones, people said.

They told her that he had said he had to go out on urgent business and would be back in the afternoon.

Star waited until four o'clock to be certain, then she headed for Kenny's counters again. He was back at work.

'I did it, Star,' he said.

'Did what?'

'Got Michael the money, like you asked.' He was very pleased to have helped her.

'How much?' She could hardly speak.

'Two thousand, like you said,' he said proudly. 'I had to go to the bank, but we got it for him in time.'

'I went to the bank today,' Shay Sullivan told them at supper. 'And I have a nice little piece of news for us all.'

'That's the first time I ever heard that going to a bank brought *good* news,' Kevin said. He and Gemma had come to discuss the plans for the Sullivan father and son setting up the much talked of health-food snack bar in the hotel's leisure complex.

'They've been overcharging you for years and now they're going to refund it?' Nick suggested. Nick was becoming a fixture in the Sullivan house with Lilly these days.

'Tell us the news, Shay,' Molly begged.

Star sat like a stone, uncaring, unhearing.

'All right, I will. When I lost interest in all that gambling thing I had one big win, remember?'

'Yes indeed, it was Small Screen that won,' said Molly. 'Everyone thought Lone Star was going to win. And you gave us all a present.'

'Well, I actually won a great deal more that day, over ten thousand euro, and someone was holding it for me. Now I've put it into the bank with an explanation of how I got it. They won't take big lumps of cash these days without knowing where it came from. And anyway, Kevin and I can now set up the business together.'

'God, that's great, Dad,' Kevin said, eyes shining.

'Well done, Mr Hale, you're home and dry.' Nick reached forward to shake him by the hand.

'Oh Shay, aren't you marvellous,' cried Molly.

Star said nothing because she hadn't been listening. So they told it to her again.

'Someone was holding it for you. I expect that was Laddy,' she said eventually.

'Well now, love, it doesn't matter who was holding it, the main thing is that it's safely in the bank,' her father said.

'Do you need it *all* for the restaurant?' Star asked in a curiously flat voice.

'And more, but it will begin to pay off in a year or two, believe me. Your brother and I are going to be tycoons.' He laughed happily.

'Could I have two thousand now, do you think?' she asked.

They all looked at her open-mouthed.

'Well, not *just* now, Star, later on, maybe. We could have a big divide-up all right, give you girls your share, and Michael of course if we ever see him again.'

'No, I really mean it, Dad, I need two thousand euro tomorrow. Please can I have it?'

'But what *for*, Star?' her mother asked. 'Why could you possibly need that kind of money?'

'It doesn't matter why, it's a secret, you all have secrets, why can't I have one?'

'It's an awful lot of money,' Lilly said.

'Not now, Star, later on, when we're up and running, if you want a car or a holiday or whatever –,' her father began.

'I don't want a car or a holiday, I just *need* that money now and I can't tell you why.' Her face, with the livid bruise on the forehead, was white and tense. The Sullivans, Gemma and Nick looked at each other in alarm.

'What could be so urgent that it can't wait?' her mother asked.

'This can't,' Star said.

'Oh my God, she wants an abortion!' Lilly cried.

'It couldn't cost all that, could it?' Gemma's eyes were enormous.

Star spoke very slowly. 'If I were to tell you that it *was* for an abortion, would you give it to me?' she asked her father.

'No, not like that. We'd need to have a

discussion, look at other possibilities,' he replied.

'This isn't something where you can just write a cheque, there are a lot of things to talk about,' her mother said. 'Like whether it would be the right thing to do, which I must say I don't think it would at all.'

'*Is* that what you need the money for?' Kevin asked.

'Why?' Star's voice was cold.

'Because one way or another it's very sad that Dad's great news has ended up in a big crisis discussion about you, as it always does. No matter what happens in this family, it's always a question of let's not upset Star.' His face was red and angry.

It was so like what Laddy had said before he went off in his van. It was so unfair, Star thought. All she had ever wanted was for everyone to be happy. And now everyone was cross with her and saying it was her fault.

CHAPTER EIGHT

WHEN STAR WENT BACK to work in the supermarket she had great plans of making it all up with Kenny. He had been put in a really bad position and it was all her fault. She had practised over and over what she would say to him. She would ask him home to supper in Chestnut Street. Everything would be all right again.

But she didn't get a chance to speak to him. Every time she approached him there seemed to be some reason that he had to hurry away. Finally she tugged at his sleeve to get his attention.

'Shouldn't you be back at your counter, Star?' he said, and she saw that his face was very cold.

Star felt as if she had swallowed a lot of iced water. Kenny was avoiding her. Kenny who had said he loved her.

She returned to the pastries and scones with her heart heavy.

*

There was a postcard from Michael when Star got home. It was addressed to the Sullivan family and it said that he was travelling for a bit and would be in touch later when things got clearer. A friend of his was posting this in Poland. It did not mean, of course, that this was where he was.

'God, that boy is getting harder to understand every day,' Shay said.

'I hope he's all right,' Molly said, worried.

'I was going to ask him to be our best man, what do you think he means by later?' Kevin asked. Kevin thought only of his wedding day the following year, and his upcoming health-food snack bar project.

Nick, who was most definitely Lilly's boyfriend now, was keen to see the best in things. 'Looks as if he has everything under control,' he said vaguely, and Lilly patted his hand.

Only Star said nothing. It was as if she was hardly listening to the conversation. There was a time when she would look from face to face, hoping that everyone was getting on well, trying to head off any trouble before it began. Not any more.

*

That night Star went and read to Miss Mack. But her voice was faltering and she had to stop. Miss Mack said they could sit and listen to music instead. Perhaps Star could put on some Haydn, she said. It would fill up your soul for you. Miss Mack's eyes were probably closed behind her dark glasses. Star sat twisting a small handkerchief until she eventually tore it into three pieces.

'Go home, child,' Miss Mack said. 'You're getting no peace from this lovely music, go home and sort it out.'

'It isn't all at home to sort out,' Star said.

'Well, go wherever it is, Star. I can hear your heart breaking from here,' said Miss Mack.

'Laddy, can I come in please?' she asked.

'No, Star, you can't.'

'I promise it will only take ten minutes.'

'Not even for ten seconds. Go home.'

But she was into the Hales' kitchen before Laddy could stop her. She took a seat opposite him as he sat reading the evening paper.

'Do you know any of Haydn's music, Laddy?' she asked.

'Nope,' he said.

'It's meant to fill your soul,' she said.

'Good,' he said, not even looking up.

'You said you liked me, once,' she said.

'Yeah.'

'So what went wrong, how did I lose you? *Tell* me, Laddy. Even if I can't get you back, I may get somebody one day, and not annoy them and drive them mad as I did with you.'

'You didn't have me to lose, stop talking crap,' he said.

'Tell me what I did wrong, then I'll leave you alone,' she begged.

For the first time he looked up. He was so handsome, she wanted to cry. 'Promise?' he said.

'Promise,' said Star Sullivan.

'Right. Where do I start? We came here to live, my dad and I. My mam had done a runner, things weren't great. Biddy was exactly what we said, a friend. She had been in some trouble and needed somewhere to stay, so she came to us. My dad fancied her, of course, but she was much too young for him and she never slept with him. She was great fun to have around the place, she kept us on our toes a bit . . . Look

101

what a mess the place is, now that she's gone.
Anyway she and I were mates too, not lovers,
not at all. Not ever. My dad was very upset
when she said she was moving on. I had just got
him persuaded that it was all for the best when
you started shouting the odds and saying that I
was having an affair with her. Now he'll never
be sure.'

'But I didn't mean –' Star began.

'You never mean anything, Star. That's your
problem.' He was very cold. 'You didn't mean it
when you asked me to help your brother,
Michael. Now I'm under heavy police suspicion
myself, even though I've never done anything
more than buy a dodgy video or DVD.'

'But I thought –'

'Sure you thought. You thought I might cure
your father's gambling. A nice man, Shay, I
always got on well with him, and now because
of you we've ended up bad friends.'

'I didn't know . . .'

'No, you never knew . . . You didn't know
that your mother looks at me as if I were the
devil out of hell, because she thinks I seduced
you when you were a child and then
abandoned you –'

'She does *not* think that!'

'Of course she does, and why not, you told the world you slept with me.'

'To save your skin.'

'Like hell. I was doing nothing, just sweeping up after your brother and his crim friends.'

'But –'

'And you go on telling me how much you want to listen to me and you never listened to one thing I said.'

'Like what?'

'Like you should tell your mother about Lilly hiding food, then she would have been helped much sooner. Like telling Michael you would shop him, then he wouldn't be on the run in Eastern Europe at this very moment.'

Star looked at him with a white face.

'And then you told that poor gobshite Kenny the Fish that I'd beaten you up and he came after me and I had to hit him. So where's the friendship in any of this, Star?'

'I didn't tell him you hit me.'

'Well, you sure didn't tell him quickly enough that I hadn't.'

'I'm so sorry.'

103

'I'm sure you are. *Now* will you go home, and remember you promised to leave me alone. You know that you promised you would.'

'All right.'

Star got up and left. She paused at the door to look back at him but he was reading the paper again.

'I brought you a cup of tea, Star,' her mother said.

'Thanks, Mam.'

'You look very sad, pet, very sad, is your head hurting?'

'No, not at all.'

'Star, what is it?'

'It's too much to tell, Mam, I've made such a mess of everything.'

'Ah, we all make a mess of most things,' Molly said soothingly.

'We don't, Mam.'

'We *do* actually, Star. We just shuffle along. No one gets it all right, the wise person knows that.'

'I don't want to get it all that right, I just want people to be happy. Is that a crime?'

'No, love, of course not, but it's just that it

won't happen. It doesn't happen. We have to put up with what we've got.'

'But I *hate* when people fight, I'd do anything on earth to avoid a row,' Star said.

'Not always the right thing to do,' her mother said.

Star thought of her brother Michael, and shivered.

'So are you are all right? Wouldn't you like to come downstairs?'

'No, Mam.'

'What are you thinking about, love?'

'I was thinking that I'd like to work somewhere else, rather than near Kenny. You know, after everything.'

'I hear he's going off to Head Office shortly,' her mother said.

'Oh.'

'So that's not a problem. What else are you worrying about?'

'My real name is Oona,' Star said.

'Of course it is, love.'

'So that's what I'm going to call myself from now on. Star hasn't worked for me, I wasn't bright enough or glittery enough, no light to shine on things. I'd like to be Oona now. In a year's time people will forget I was ever called Star.'

'All right, sweetheart,' her mother said. It was just one more thing to cope with in the day.

And in a year's time when Oona Sullivan won the Employee of the Year Award in the supermarket chain, it was Kenny, the Area Manager, who presented it. He was astounded to find it was the girl he knew as Star. He had never guessed it was the same person.

And when she was bridesmaid at Gemma and Kevin's wedding, her picture was in the evening paper as Ms Oona Sullivan, sister of the groom.

And she got a postcard from Laddy who now lived far away. It said: 'Welcome to the real world, Oona Sullivan. May you be much happier and much nicer than all those silly little stars.'

And because she was so grown up now, Oona smiled and was pleased, rather than thinking, as the old Star would have done, that the love of her life was on his way back to her.

WORLD BOOK DAY
Quick Reads

We would like to thank all our partners on the *Quick* Reads project for all their help and support:

BBC RaW
Department for Education and Skills
Trades Union Congress
The Vital Link
The Reading Agency
National Literacy Trust

Quick Reads would also like to thank the Arts Council England and National Book Tokens for their sponsorship.

We would also like to thank the following companies for providing their services free of charge: SX Composing for typesetting all the titles; Icon Reproduction for text reproduction; Norske Skog, Stora Enso, PMS and Iggusend for paper/board supplies; Mackays of Chatham, Cox and Wyman, Bookmarque, White Quill Press, Concise, Norhaven and GGP for the printing.

www.worldbookday.com

Quick Reads

BOOKS IN THE *Quick* Reads SERIES

The Book Boy	Joanna Trollope
Blackwater	Conn Iggulden
Chickenfeed	Minette Walters
Don't Make Me Laugh	Patrick Augustus
Hell Island	Matthew Reilly
How to Change Your Life in 7 Steps	John Bird
Screw It, Let's Do It	Richard Branson
Someone Like Me	Tom Holt
Star Sullivan	Maeve Binchy
The Team	Mick Dennis
The Thief	Ruth Rendell
Woman Walks into a Bar	Rowan Coleman

AND IN MAY 2006

Cleanskin	Val McDermid
Danny Wallace and the Centre of the Universe	Danny Wallace
Desert Claw	Damien Lewis
The Dying Wish	Courttia Newland
The Grey Man	Andy McNab
I Am a Dalek	Garath Roberts
I Love Football	Hunter Davies
The Name You Once Gave Me	Mike Phillips
The Poison in the Blood	Tom Holland
Winner Takes All	John Francome

Look out for more titles in the *Quick* Reads series in 2007.

www.worldbookday.com

Have you enjoyed reading this
Quick **Reads book?**

Would you like to read more?

Or learn how to write fantastically?

If so, you might like to attend a course to
develop your skills.

Courses are **free** and available in your local area.

If you'd like to find out more,
phone **0800 100 900**.

You can also ask for a **free video or DVD** showing
other people who have been on our courses and
the changes they have made in their lives.

Don't get by – get on.

Don't get by get on 0800 100 900

FIRST CHOICE BOOKS

If you enjoyed this book, you'll find more great reads on www.firstchoicebooks.org.uk. First Choice Books allows you to search by type of book, author and title. So, whether you're looking for romance, sport, humour – or whatever turns you on – you'll be able to find other books you'll enjoy.

You can also borrow books from your local library. If you tell them what you've enjoyed, they can recommend other good reads they think you will like.

First Choice is part of the Vital Link, promoting reading for pleasure. To find out more about the Vital Link visit www.vitallink.org.uk

RaW

Find out what the BBC's RaW (Reading and Writing) campaign has to offer at www.bbc.co.uk/raw

NEW ISLAND

New Island publishers have produced four series of books in its Open Door series – brilliant short novels for adults from the cream of Irish writers. Visit www.newisland.ie and go to the Open Door section.

SANDSTONE PRESS

In the Sandstone Vista Series, Sandstone Press Ltd publish quality contemporary fiction and non-fiction books. The full list can be found at their website www.sandstonepress.com.

Quick Reads

The Book Boy by Joanna Trollope

Bloomsbury

Sometimes it takes a stranger to guess a family secret.

Alice has a house, a husband, two children and a part-time job. She ought to be happy but she isn't because she has a secret which is never talked about in the family: she can't read.

But Alice decides to take charge of her life and change it with the help of the strangest companion – the book boy.

Quick Reads

The Thief by Ruth Rendell

Arrow

Stealing from people who had upset her was something Polly did quite a lot. There was her Aunt Pauline, a girl at school, a boyfriend who had left her. And there was the man on the plane . . .

Humiliated and scared by a total stranger, Polly does what she always does: she steals something. But she never could have imagined that her desire for revenge would have such terrifying results.

Quick Reads

Blackwater by Conn Iggulden

HarperCollins

Blackwater is a cold, dark thriller with a twist.

Davey has always lived in the shadow of his older brother, who will stop at nothing to protect himself and his family. But when Denis Tanter comes into Davey's life, how far will they go to get him out of trouble?

How far can you go before you're in too deep?

Quick Reads

Woman Walks into a Bar by Rowan Coleman

Arrow

Twenty-eight-year-old single mother Sam spends her days working in the local supermarket and her Friday nights out with her friends. Life has never been easy for Sam, but she's always hoped one day she'll meet 'The One'.

She's starting to lose hope when her friends set her up on a blind date. At first Sam's horrified, but then she agrees – after all, you never know when you might meet the man of your dreams . . .

Quick Reads

Don't Make Me Laugh by Patrick Augustus

The X Press

It's not funny. Leo and Trevor are twins, but
they hate each other's guts. Leo says his brother
got off with his woman. Trevor reckons it was
the other way round. Only Mum can stop them
ripping each other to bits. But HER big secret is
that one of them has to die.

Quick Reads

Screw It, Let's Do It by Richard Branson

Virgin

Learn the secrets of a global icon.

Throughout my life I have strived for success – as a businessman, in my adventures, as an author and a proud father and husband. I want to share the many truths I've learned along the road to success which have helped me to be the best I can. They include:

Have faith in yourself
Believe that anything can be done
Don't let other people put you off
Never give up

Learn these and other simple truths, and I hope you will be inspired to get the most out of your life and to achieve your goals. People will try to talk you out of ideas and say, 'It can't be done,' but if you have faith in yourself you'll find you can achieve almost anything.